LEROY THE LABRADOR
The Big Move

Allyson Roberts

Illustrations by Irena Romendik

MAXIMUM POTENTIAL, INC.

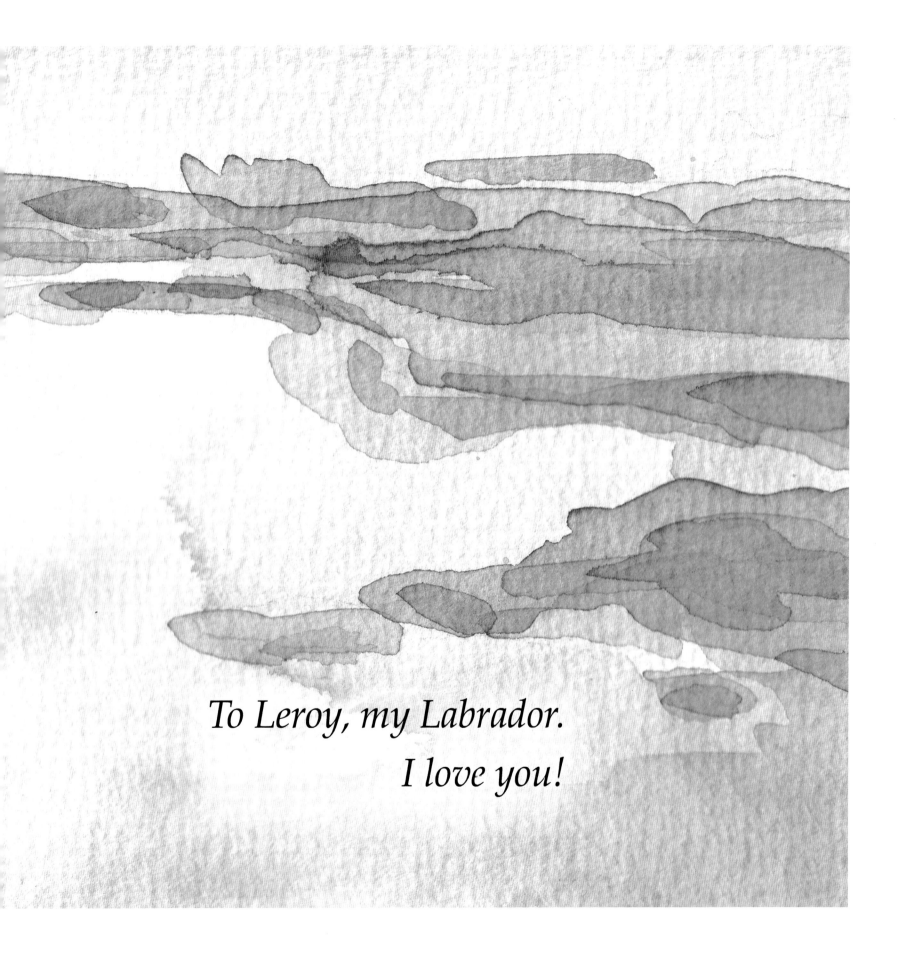

To Leroy, my Labrador.
I love you!

Maximum Potential, Inc.
Leroy the Labrador—The Big Move
Copyright © 2005 by Allyson Roberts

For further information, contact the author at:
10525 Wren Ridge Road, Alpharetta, GA 30022
PH: 714-392-2001
allycat4365@aol.com

Book design by:
The Floating Gallery
www.thefloatinggallery.com

Allyson Roberts
Leroy the Labrador—The Big Move

1. Author 2. Title 3. Children's Book

ISBN: 0-9759305-1-6
LCCN: 2004118025
Printed in China

LEROY THE LABRADOR

The Big Move

Hi! My name is Leroy the Labrador. But some people just call me "the dog." I have a name...they should use it. Leroy. See how it rolls off the tongue?

Just because I am a dog, many people think that I don't have feelings. Since you are young, I bet that sometimes you feel that way, too. I know that my human mommy and daddy don't always understand when I am sad. Do I have to wear a sign?

Anyway, I want to share a story with you about my big move to a new house. I felt scared and lonely. My family suspected that I would not want to move, but no one consulted "the dog."

It was a regular day. I woke up, watched my daddy leave for work, and then sat down with my mommy to read a story. She read from a book about a dog that flies a plane. I loved that story! All dogs should get to fly a plane. The goggles are real cool.

After my story I played outside in the yard. It was my favorite place in the whole wide world. I sniffed grass, chased butterflies and rested in the sun. Mommy and Daddy say that my fur glistens in the sunlight and that I look beautiful lying in it. All I know is that I felt good. The sun was warm. It made me happy.

Later that same afternoon, Mommy took me to Puppy Kindergarten, where I learned to sit, stay and shake hands. What is the obsession with shaking hands? In Japan they bow. I prefer bowing. It's very classy.

After the class was over, I heard Mommy say something about moving to my teacher. I did not understand at the time what this "moving" meant.

But it was my first clue.

Then my teacher said that the "new school" was wonderful and I would make lots of new friends. I did not want new friends. I wanted my same friends. My best friends Annie and Linus played with me at Kindergarten every week. Why did I need new friends?

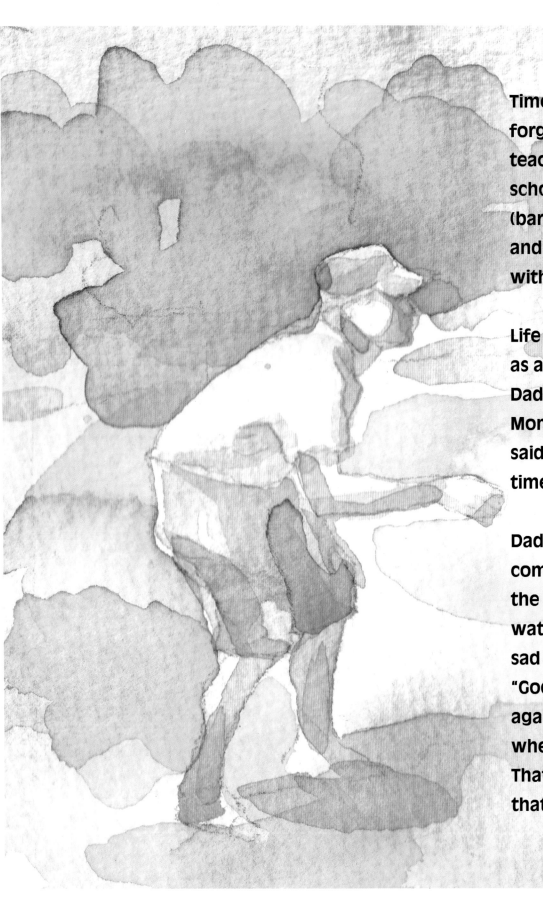

Time went by and I soon forgot about what my teacher had said that day at school. I was very busy (barking, sniffing, sleeping) and couldn't be bothered with details.

Life at home was wonderful, as always. Then one day Daddy took me to the park. Mommy did not come. She said she needed "alone time."

Daddy and I practiced my commands over and over in the park while people watched us. Daddy had a sad look in his eyes. He said, "Good boy" over and over again. It's never a good sign when he repeats himself. That was my second clue that something was up.

I love my daddy. He is the best daddy in the whole wide world. We always spend special time together and he says "good boy" a lot. I like it when he tells me that I am good.

My Daddy also gives me treats when we practice what I learn at Puppy Kindergarten. I sit, stay, shake hands...real simple stuff, but it makes him happy. He's big on saying, "Heel, Leroy. Heel!"

Our time at the park ended as soon as it began. Daddy said we needed to head back home. When we pulled into the driveway, there were cars everywhere. I wondered what was going on.

When we went inside, there were boxes everywhere. Our friends were packing up our television. That's right — the TV!

This was the big clue!

Mommy rushed around serving pizza and drinks. I begged for a piece but no one paid attention. How obvious did I have to be?

People were rushing everywhere. Some of them would walk by me and pet my head. I felt afraid and happy at the same time. Something very strange was going on inside our house.

Mommy came over to me and showed me a box. Inside the box were all my special toys. My tail began to wag uncontrollably. It's a compulsion.

I have the best toys! Some of them are in shreds because I like to chew a lot. They are still my favorites. Mommy was holding up my toys one at a time, saying, "See, Leroy, here is Binkie. I am putting him in this special box for you. Here is Lester! He goes in here, too. We cannot forget your special things."

My stomach felt strange like I ate too much pepperoni. Why were things being put into boxes? Were they going to put me into a box?

Soon the house was empty. Mommy and Daddy were tired, too. They motioned for me to come into their room, as always. I used to sleep in my tiny corner of the room all snuggled up in a blanket on the floor beside my parents.

Daddy snored really loud in the middle of the night. I woke up and pretended that an elephant came to our house. Daddy's nose sounded just like an elephant's trunk bellowing.

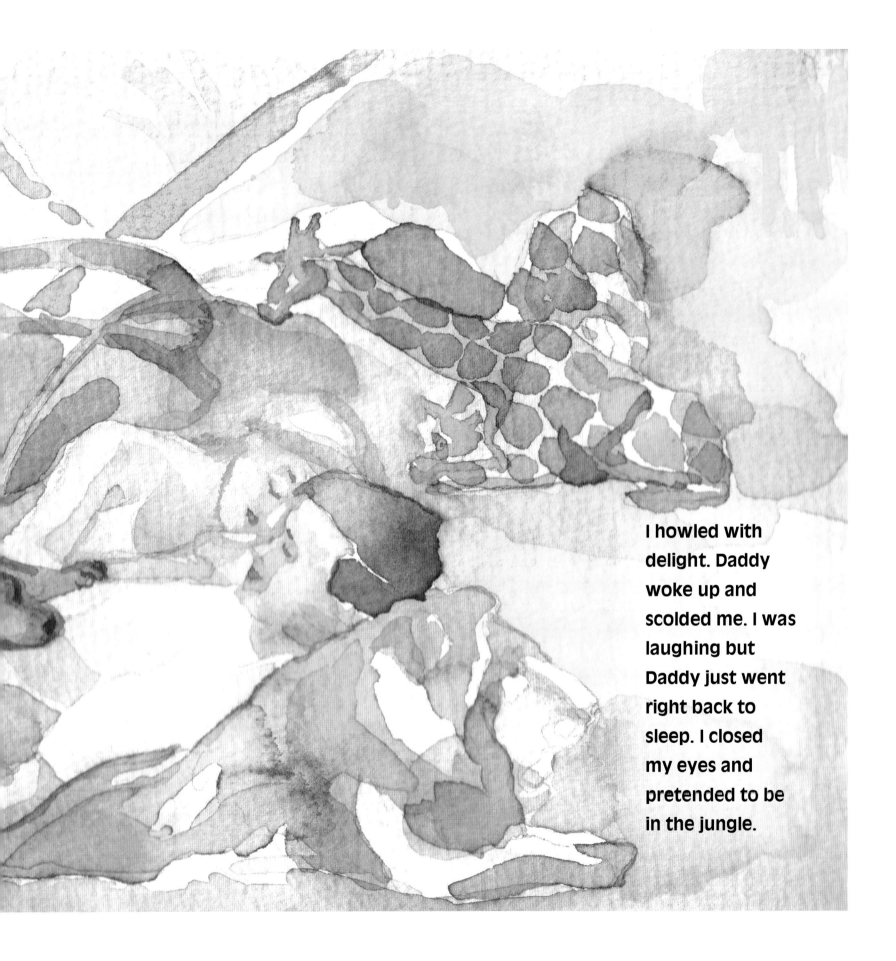

I howled with delight. Daddy woke up and scolded me. I was laughing but Daddy just went right back to sleep. I closed my eyes and pretended to be in the jungle.

The next morning, I woke up late. I could hear a loud engine outside. At first I thought it was a fire truck, but it was another type of truck. Two men were taking all of our furniture from inside our house and putting it into the back of the truck. I barked at them to stop, but everyone was telling me to calm down.

You can never know for sure if you are really being robbed, so I barked for a few more minutes just to let everyone know I was on the job.

Then Mommy held up in her hand a special bag that I had never seen before. She called me to her side and said, "See, Leroy, here are your bones, chew toys, special treats and inflatable bowl for your water."

Daddy said, "We're all going to take a nice drive. Mommy, too."

Hooray, I thought. Everyone's going to the park. We're even bringing my toys this time!"

Mommy and Daddy loaded me into the car. Mommy never came on park trips, so I was a little confused. What happened to her "alone time"?

We drove for a longer time than I can ever remember. Past my favorite fire hydrant, past the school, past the park, past...everything.

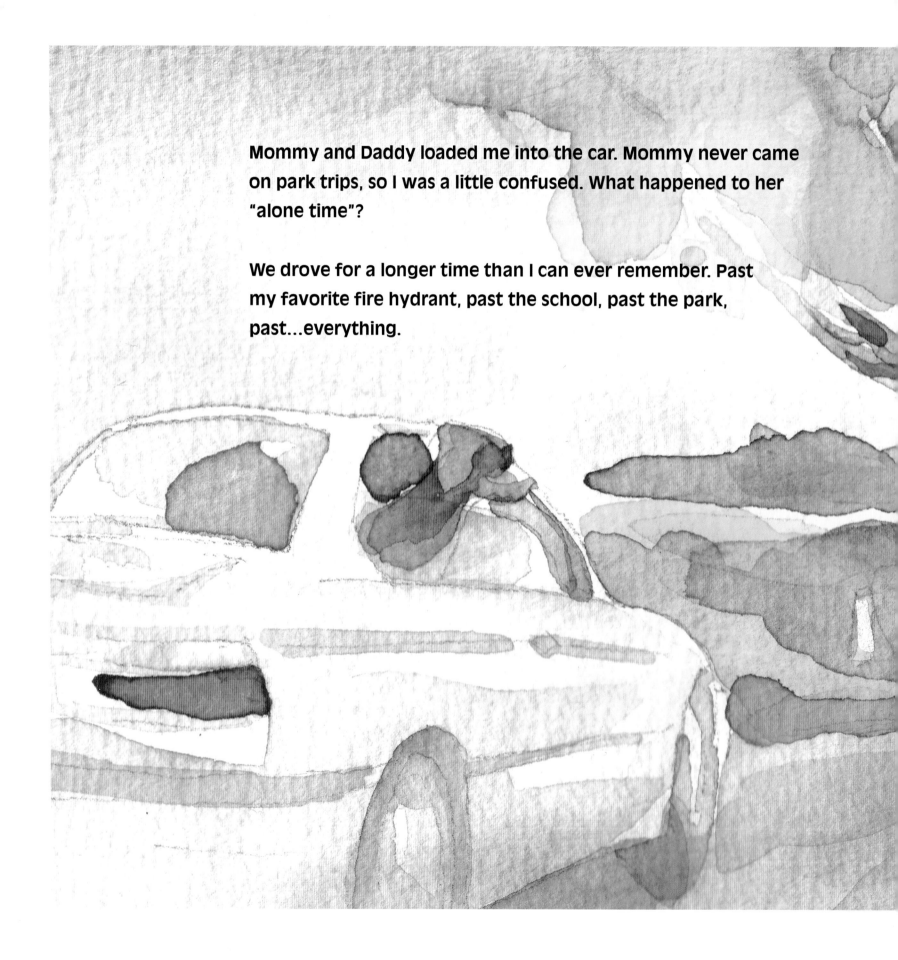

Where were we going?

Mommy and Daddy kept petting my head and saying, "Here we go, Leroy!" and "Good boy, Leroy!"

Even though I was nervous, I managed to smile. I love it when I am called a good boy because I work very hard at it. You can't imagine the amount of study and devotion it takes!

Mommy pulled out my special bag and placed it in front of me. I chewed on some of my toys. It felt good to have my things with me.

After a few potty breaks and a stop for lunch, we finally arrived at another house. This house was much bigger than our house. The yard was also bigger and there were plants and flowers everywhere! Mommy and Daddy jumped out of our car and started giving orders to the men to take our furniture into the new house.

What a strange game!

I wandered into the new house not knowing what to think. Every room was empty. Why were we bringing our things into this strange place?

Just then Mommy wrapped her long, beautiful arms around my neck. "Leroy, come here, boy!" she said.

I followed Mommy down a long hallway and into another room. Inside this room were some things I had never seen before. There was a bed with my name on it and a pillow with black paws just like mine. On the other side of the room was the box that Mommy and Daddy had shown me the night before. I knew my special things were in that box. Mommy and Daddy had packed my special things for me to have here!

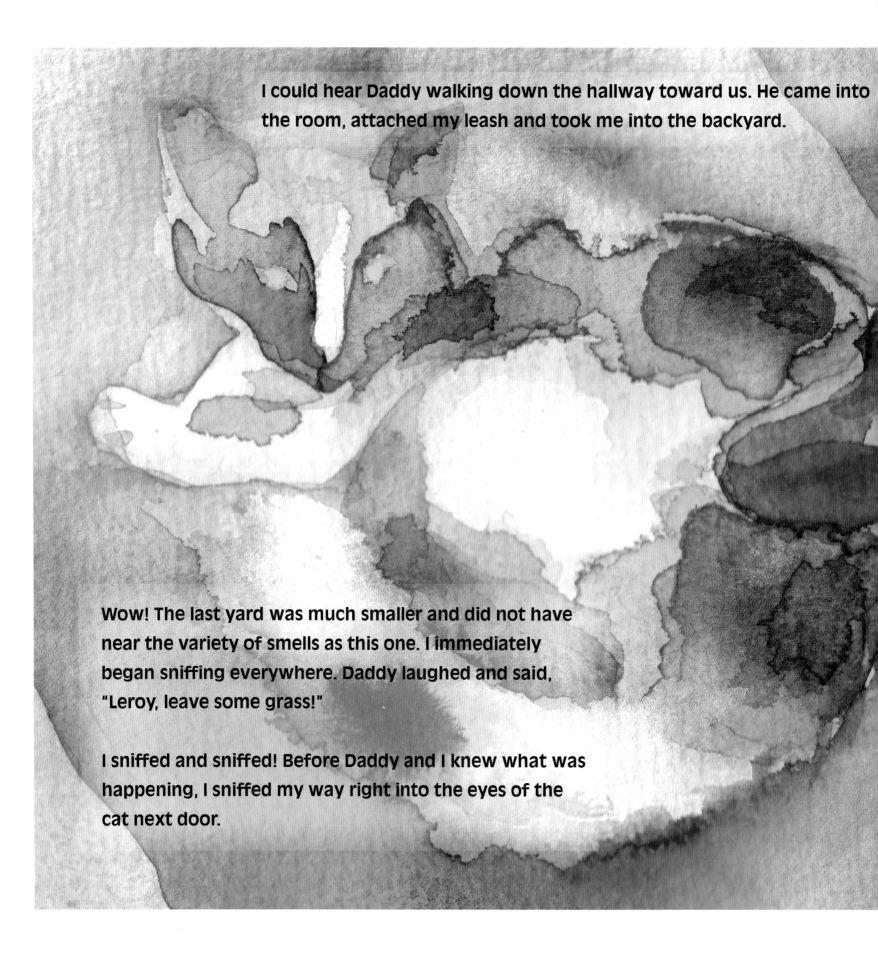

I could hear Daddy walking down the hallway toward us. He came into the room, attached my leash and took me into the backyard.

Wow! The last yard was much smaller and did not have near the variety of smells as this one. I immediately began sniffing everywhere. Daddy laughed and said, "Leroy, leave some grass!"

I sniffed and sniffed! Before Daddy and I knew what was happening, I sniffed my way right into the eyes of the cat next door.

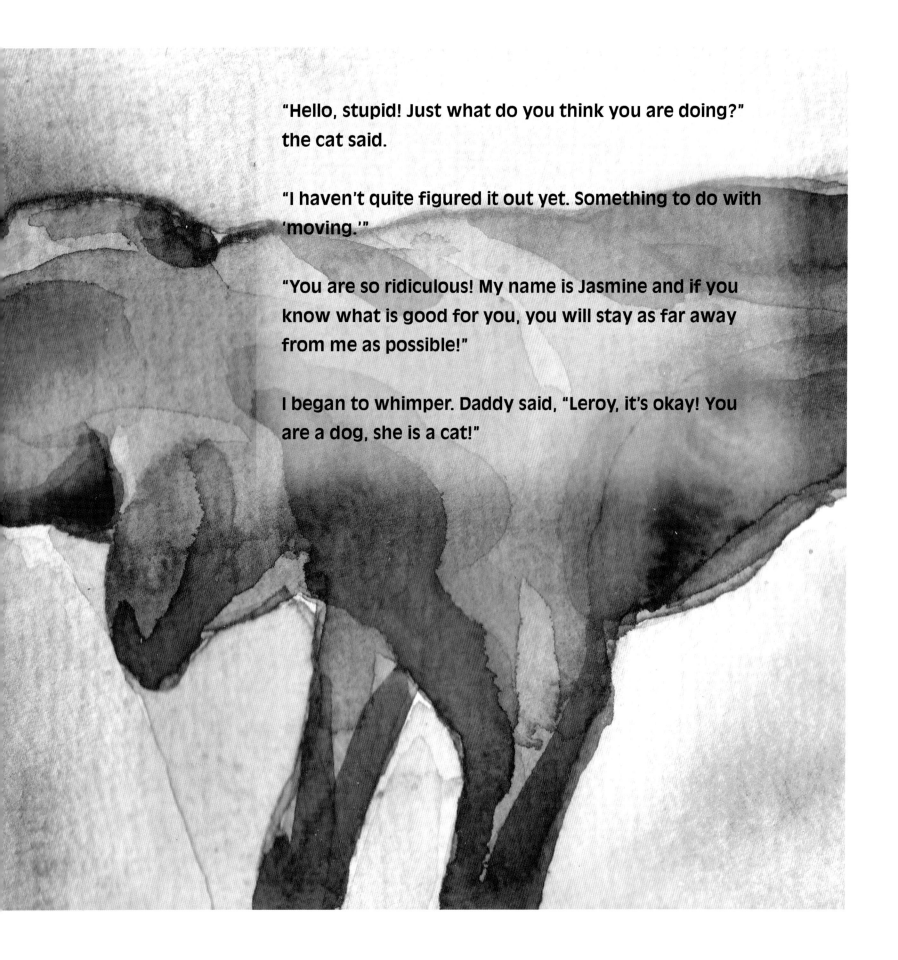

"Hello, stupid! Just what do you think you are doing?" the cat said.

"I haven't quite figured it out yet. Something to do with 'moving.'"

"You are so ridiculous! My name is Jasmine and if you know what is good for you, you will stay as far away from me as possible!"

I began to whimper. Daddy said, "Leroy, it's okay! You are a dog, she is a cat!"

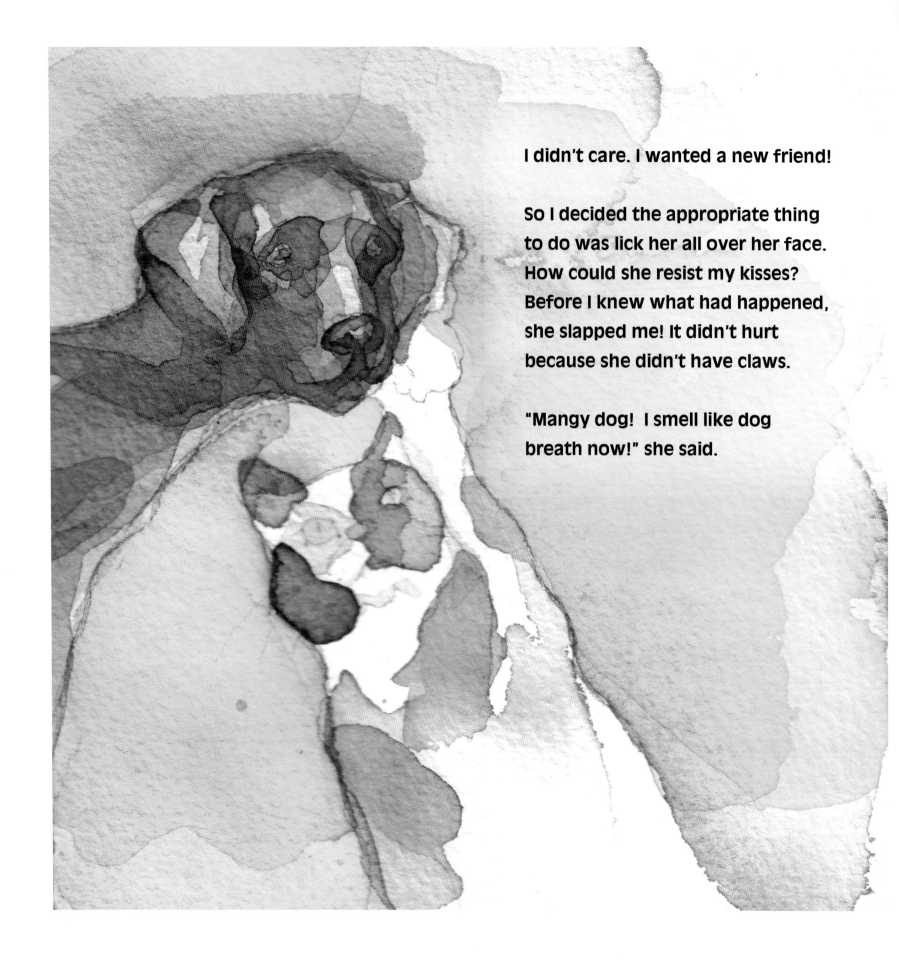

I didn't care. I wanted a new friend!

So I decided the appropriate thing to do was lick her all over her face. How could she resist my kisses? Before I knew what had happened, she slapped me! It didn't hurt because she didn't have claws.

"Mangy dog! I smell like dog breath now!" she said.

I laughed and laughed until my stomach ached. Daddy was laughing, too. Jasmine was licking herself clean and giving me angry looks. Mommy ran outside to find what the commotion was all about. Daddy told her about Jasmine and me.

They laughed together and began to pet Jasmine and tell her that I was not all that bad. She didn't believe it for a minute. I really wanted to be friends with her. I hoped she would grow to like me.

As the days went by, I wondered when the men would come back and take our furniture back to our old house. The new house was very nice but I missed my friends Annie and Linus.

Then it slowly began to dawn on me...we were not going back home. This was our home.

So...this was moving.

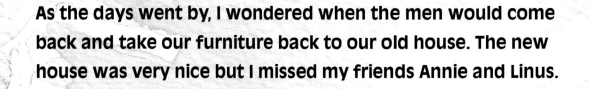

I couldn't help but cry a little bit. My nose became snuffled and it was hard to breathe. I looked up to see Mommy and Daddy standing over me. They dropped to their knees at the same time. Before I could resist, both of them were hugging me tightly.

Mommy said, "Leroy, we thought you would want your own room with puppies painted on the wall."

Daddy said, "Yes! We also thought you would love the big backyard where all of us could spend time together with our friends. Beyond the yard is a duck pond. Mommy and Daddy thought you would love swimming and chasing the ducks around the pond! We know you miss your friends. We are sorry, Leroy!"

My own room? Painted puppies on the wall? A duck pond? It was all very exciting but I still missed my friends. They would have loved to play with me in the pond.

I had cried enough, though, and so I ran behind Daddy, who was already to the backdoor, coaxing me to follow him.

Ducks, here we come!

Over time I settled into my new home. Jasmine and I slowly became friends. She kept calling me "Precious," but I could tell that she did not really mean it.

Daddy and I played in the duck pond almost every afternoon. We even played in the rain and Mommy did not like that one bit. She made me wipe my paws off over and over before Daddy and I could come back inside.

I also loved my new room. Mommy had lived up to her promise and I had Labrador puppies painted all over my new bedroom walls. At first I was afraid at night, but I could still hear Daddy's snores so I was okay.

One day while playing in the backyard
with Jasmine — she hid up in a tree and
I barked at her — I suddenly realized I
wasn't the only one barking.

The backdoor of my house swung open
and there stood my two best friends
in the whole wide world — Annie and
Linus. I could not believe my eyes! I
ran to them and we jumped all over
each other.

Our mommies were laughing and finally they went back inside. I took my friends to the duck pond where we chased ducks and swam all day. Jasmine followed us and she and I told the story about the first day we met. Annie and Linus laughed and Jasmine could finally laugh, too.

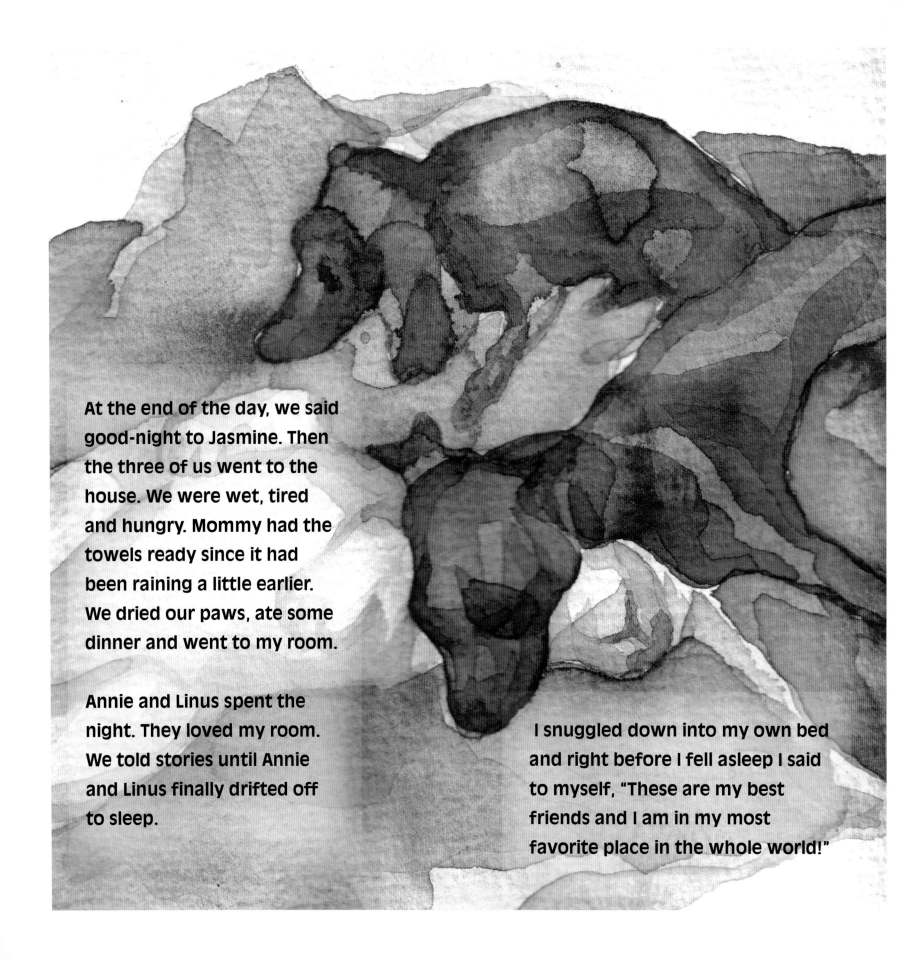

At the end of the day, we said good-night to Jasmine. Then the three of us went to the house. We were wet, tired and hungry. Mommy had the towels ready since it had been raining a little earlier. We dried our paws, ate some dinner and went to my room.

Annie and Linus spent the night. They loved my room. We told stories until Annie and Linus finally drifted off to sleep.

I snuggled down into my own bed and right before I fell asleep I said to myself, "These are my best friends and I am in my most favorite place in the whole world!"